ANGELS IN DISGUISE

ANGELS IN DISGUISE

Raymond Soto

To order additional copies of this book, contact:
Xlibris Corporation
1-888-795-4274
www.Xlibris.com
Orders@Xlibris.com
50084

Our story opens in Beverly Hills, the land of milk and honey. For some the milk turns sour and for others the honey is too high to reach.

This story is about three wealthy men who are tired of the rat race in Beverly Hills. There is EDDY, a director for Viejo Pictures in Hollywood. He has won many awards and has screwed up many motion pictures, too. There is LEACH, a producer of many movies. And there is AL, a critic, the best in town. He's won 27 awards and that's nothing to snivel at.

Three wealthy men, tired of the rat race and due for a change.

Al and Leach are on their way to Eddy's office. Al arrives first, opens the door to Eddy's office and says, "Eddy, how are you?"

Eddy:	"Hey Al, what are you up to? Ready for that vacation?"
Al:	"Goddamn right. I've *been* ready for this vacation. You know, I feel this vacation is going to be something special."
Eddy:	"You're damn right! We've never done anything like this before. We've always been stuck here in Beverly Hills. He looks at his watch. "What the hell is keeping Leach? He "should have been here by now."
Al:	"He probably stopped to see that whore again."

Leach walks in and says, "Let's get this show on the road, men," setting down a six pack of Bud and handing each of them a beer. "I'm all packed and ready to go."

Eddy:	"Hell, we've got two more days left. We're not leaving till Friday."
Leach:	"Well, I'm anxious to get there and meet that little country girl."
Al:	"So am I. That's the reason we're all going, right? To meet that country girl and get married. I don't want to marry a girl here in Beverly Hills; they all shit on you. Everybody's in the fast lane here."
Eddy:	"Don't worry, we'll meet those country girls alright. Of course we're leaving our Cadillacs and Mercedes here. We'll buy some junk cars over there. We don't want the girls to know we're millionaires. They'll just marry us for our money."
Al:	"*All right!* That's a good idea. Now I've got an idea. Let's pick up the girls and paint the town red before we go."

Leach: "That's great. Let's all meet at Chasen's tomorrow night.

The next night they pick up their lady friends and meet at Chasen's. They meet at the bar to have a few drinks and do some bullshitting before dinner. They have dinner, dance, and go to their own apartments with their lady friends. The next day they all wake up with hangovers and slowly make their way through the early afternoon, saying goodbye to their friends since they're going to be away for a year. They all agree to meet at Eddy's place and leave in one car.

Al: "Wowee! That's quite a load. How long did you say it would take to get to this town we're going to?
Eddy: "Just taking our time we'll be there in four hours."
Leach: "Well, let's get the hell out of here."

They drive south on Beverly Drive, turn left on Fairfax and right on Sunset toward the freeway. On their way down Sunset they smile and wave to the ladies of the street.

Eddy: "There's China Doll." He smiles. "She's a good kid."

Halfway down the block Leach calls, "Rebecca, how ya doin'?"

Rebecca: "Great. How ya doin'?

Leach gives her an O.K. sign with a doubled up fist.

Al: "I don't see Gina around . . ." He looks around. " . . . She's probably busy.

They come to the freeway entrance and head north.
Al says to Eddy who is driving, "Drive on Maestro," and their journey begins. Two hundred miles north of Beverly Hills they pass Santa Barbara, and a few miles down the road they gas up in Bullton and take off again. They come to San Luis Obispo and check in at the Madonna Inn Restaurant & Motel. Eddy's chauffeur, TONY, has just checked out. He got there a couple of days ahead to drive the car back to Beverly Hills.

Tony: "How are you, Mr. Moreno (Eddy), Mr. Morgan (Leach), Mr. Strosiky?" Al.

"Real good—fine—great, great," they answer.

Leach: "How's this little town, Tony?"
Tony: "From what I've seen it's fantastic. You have everything here, fishing, hunting, boating, shooting . . ."

As he's talking this beautiful, sexy lady passes by and gets in her Mercedes Benz, showing all kinds of beautiful leg.

Leach: "Tell me, Tony, did you get any while you were here? Just smile if you did."

Tony smiles and laughs in a low voice.

Leach: "You hound dog."

Eddy and Al also smile and laugh in a low voice

Eddy: "Here's the keys to the car, Tony. If any of the girls want to ride anywhere, take them anywhere they want to go."
Tony: "Yes sir, Mr. Moreno. You gentlemen have a good vacation."

"Will do—sure thing—right on," they say and they register.
Leach is the last one to register and says to the lady desk clerk, "Is the restaurant still open?"

Lady desk clerk:"Yes, it's open till 1 A.M."

They order their sandwiches and are all eating.

Leach: "I wonder what kind of a job I should get?"
Al: "I don't know about you but I'm going to get a job as a waiter. How about you, Eddy?"
Eddy: "I'm not sure . . . anything that comes along, I guess."
Leach: "I think I'll try bartending. I'm a hell of a barkeep. I've tended bar a lot at my private parties."
Eddy: "First thing in the morning I'm going to get me a car."
Al: "What kind of a car are you going to get, Eddy?"
Eddy: "Just so it's a junky car. That's all I'm interested in. I've never had a junky car."

Al:	"None of us have. Hey, this is going to be fun. I think I'll get me a junky car, too."
Leach:	"Three junky cars coming up in the morning, and they laugh about it . . ."
Eddy:	"I guess I'll get me an apartment somewhere tomorrow."
Leach:	"Yeah, let's call it a day."

The next day Leach finds an apartment in Morrow Bay, about twelve miles north of San Luis Obispo. He has already bought his car, a '75 Ford, and has gotten a job as a bartender at the Hungry Tiger.

Al has landed a job at the motel, barbecuing steaks and ribs and found a small house in San Luis Obispo.

Edddy gets a job in Avila at the San Luis Bay Inn as a maintenance man and buys a pickup and camper. That way he can see more of the area day' or night. Eddy, Leach and Al have been on the job about four days now.

Leach is tending bar and has just opened when a beautiful lady walks in and says, "How about pouring me the biggest Margarita you've got?"

Leach:	"One large Margarita coming up." As he's mixing the drink he says, "How are you this beautiful morning?"

The lady says, "I won't know till after I drink that Margarita."
Leach smiles and says, "Rough night or rough morning?"
The lady just lights her cigarette and says, "How about a rough year?"

Leach:	"That's bad huh."
Lady:	"It's my husband. He's an asshole. He drives me to drink."

A waitress walks in a orders a Brandy Alexander and a martini.

Waitress:	"How are you doing this morning, Leach?"
Leach:	"Pretty good. So far, Sandy's got a party coming in at twelve that'll keep me busy till one thirty . . . How's your mom, Sandy?"
Sandy:	"She's still very sick, getting worse every day."
Leach:	"Don't worry about it, Sandy. I'm sure she'll start feeling better soon." He gives her the drinks and says, "That's six dollars, Sandy." Two customers come in and Leach serves them two Budweiser beers and starts to cut up limes.

The lady says, "What time does your shift end?"

Leach: "I've still got quite a ways to go—six o'clock."

The lady looks at her watch and says, "Oh, I've got to go. I'm late." She takes a last sip and leaves.

Leach: "That's what's wrong with this world. Everyone's in a hurry."

Eddy is getting supplies in the storeage room at work when a beautiful lady walks in and starts to fix a vase of flowers.

Eddy: "Hello, beautiful. What's your name?"
Lady: "Clara. What's yours?"
Eddy: "Eddy. I haven't seen you around before."
Clara: "I've been off for two days. How long have you worked here?"
Eddy: "This is my fourth day."
Clara: "You like it?"
Eddy: "Yes, it seems very pleasant to work here . . . I like working with beautiful women."

Clara just smiles.
Terry, another maid, walks in and says, "Eddy, I need you to move a couch for me. Will you please help me?"

Eddy: "Sure, let me take these supplies to the bar and I'll meet you in the lobby. Clara, what's for lunch? Do you know?"
Clara: "Somebody said meat loaf."
Eddy: "Huh, sounds pretty good. See you at lunch?"

He takes the supplies to the bar and meets Terry in the lobby. They take the elevator to the fourth floor. On their way to the fourth floor Terry says, "I've sure got a bad hangover this morning."

Eddy: "Terry, you don't look like the type that drinks."
Terry: "I don't. My boyfriend left me so I tied one on."
Eddy: "Thats too bad, Terry. But you'll get over it."
Terry: "I'm already over it."

Eddy smiles. "A few drinks will do it every time, huh?"

Terry: "You're telling me."

The elevator door opens and they step out. On their way down the hall a lady comes toward them with her seven year old son, saying, "Here, son, you behave when we get to the dining room and don't be throwing things around like you did yesterday, you hear?"

The boy nods his head yes.

Terry stands in front of the door looking for the key on her keychain. Eddy looks at the lady and the boy who are standing in front of the elevator. The boy gives Eddy the finger and they walk into the elevator.

Eddy: "Did you see that? That kid gave me the finger."

Terry laughs and opens the door. "Oh come on. He's only about seven."

Eddy: "A seven year old monster. That's what he is."
Terry: "I need this couch over here and the T.V. here."

Eddy moves the couch and T.V. and sits down. He says, "Terry, what makes a woman like you so beautiful and sexy?"

Terry: "Eddy, I bet you say that to all the girls, don't you?"
Eddy: "Yeah, I do . . . Let me buy you a drink after work."

Terry looks at him for about four seconds and says, "*Alright.*"

That night they meet at a quiet little bar and talk, joke and dance. It's now a quarter to ten.

Terry: "Eddy, if I tell you something, you won't get mad?"
Eddy: "Of course not. What is it?"
Terry: "I have to leave."
Eddy: "Leave?!"
Terry: "My mother is confined to a wheelchair and most of the time I have to help her get to bed around this time."
Eddy: "Well, it's more important to look after your mom."
Terry: "Thanks, Eddy, I knew you'd understand." She kisses him on the cheek and says, "See you at work." She leaves.

Eddy watches her leave and says in a low voice, "*Well, shit.*" He finishes the rest of his drink in one gulp and goes to the cigarette machine to get cigarettes.

On his way out he hears a lady on the phone saying, "You mean it'll be half an hour before you can send a cab here? . . . Alright, alright, I'll be here."

Eddy: "Excuse me, could I give you a lift?"
Lady: "Who are you?"
Eddy: "My name's Eddy and I come here all the time. Ask the waitress. I'm not a nut."
Lady: "Well, I don't want to put you out of your way."
Eddy: "No bother. Where do you live?"
Lady: "Out on Spyglass Point."
Eddy: "My truck's out in front." When she gets in the truck she shows quite a bit of leg. Eddy says, "Did your car break down?"
Lady: "No, I don't have a car. I took a cab. I was supposed to meet some guy at old, port, but I guess I got stood up."

Eddy just glances at her and keeps driving.

Eddy: "What's your name?"
Lady: "Doris. Doris Francois."
Eddy: "You're French."
Doris: "Yes, I am. Turn right at the next ramp then left. It's the last house on the right."
Eddy: "All right . . . well, here you are."
Doris: "Thank you very much, Eddy. I really appreciate the lift. Have a good night."
Eddy: "Ahhh . . . aren't you going to ask me in?"
Doris: " . . . Sure, come on in." They go into the house. Doris says, "Can I get you a beer?"
Eddy: "Thank you. How long have you lived in this area, Doris?"
Doris: "All my life. I feel like moving away to some place I've never been to. I guess everybody does that sooner or later."
Eddy: "Yeah, I guess they do."

She hands him a beer and turns the stereo on.

Doris: "You like that slow music?"
Eddy: "Yes, I do. It's very nice music."

She sits on the couch with him and talks about her job as a waitress and his job as a maintenance man. About half an hour later Doris says, "Could I get you another beer?"

EDDY

Another beer is not what I need.

DORES

(stares at him for about 3 seconds)
What is it that you need?

Eddy scootes closer to her and kisses her softly and rubs her thighs then they both embrace and he leans her back on the couch. They kiss for a few seconds.

DORES

Ohhh, I need you.

Eddy picks her up and takes her to the bedroom. He lays her on the bed and kisses her thighs and then he unbuttons her blouse.

AL

Jennie, we're off in ten minutes. You want to have a drink with me.

JENNIE

You bet. I'll need more than one.

AL

I got some extra ribs left over so we can have a bite before that drink.

JENNIE

I'll need more than one rib too.

Al just smiles at her, finished his last order and called the bar.

AL

This is Al, Jerry have the waitress bring me two Buds and put them on my bill. Have her leave them on the order window. Thanks Jerry.

He gets the ribs and takes them to the back room where the employees take their breaks. He changed his clothes in the dressing room. When he came back he picked up their two Buds and goes to the break room where Jennie is already eating.

AL

This Bud's for me, this one's for you.

JENNIE

These ribs are really good Al.

AL

Of course.

JENNIE

Are you bragging?

AL

(smiles)
Of course.

JENNIE

Oh the manager asked me to tell you if you would go to Tascadero tomorrow before you come to work and pick up a box of ribs tomorrow before you come to work. Here's the address.

15

AL

Yeah, I guess I could . . . what happened to the delivery man?

JENNIE

They said he got in a wreck.

AL

Let's get that drink, Jennie.

JENNIE

Let me change and I'll meet you in the bar.

They drank and danced and talked with other friends.

JENNIE

I have to go now Al, it's getting late.

AL

Yeah I'm going to call it a day too. Could I give you a lift?

JENNIE

No, I got my car. I'll see you tomorrow afternoon.

AL

Goodnight, Jennie.

Al woke up late the next morning, looked at the clock.

AL

Oh, shit.

He showers and has a quick breakfast and off to get the ribs. It was a nice sunny day. He saw some deer on the countryside. Further down was a herd of cattle on a ranch. He takes the off ramp into the town of Tascadero. He sees a cab on a side street and pulls over to it.

AL

Excuse me, Sir, can you tell me where 1228 Los Arbollis Road is?

CAB DRIVER

Yeah, stay on this street to the dead end, turn left, then right and it'll be on your right hand side.

AL

Thank you Sir.

He drives to the wholesale meat warehouse and enters the front office.

AL

Good afternoon, Miss. My name's Al. I came to pick up a box of ribs for the motel inn.

GIRL

Oh yes, the order was phoned in this morning. I'll have Karen help you.

She presses a button on the intercom.

GIRL

Karen, you have a customer in the front office. She'll be right with you Sir.

AL

Thank you.

A few minutes pass. Karen enters the office.

GIRL

Al needs a case of ribs.

Al and Karen look at each other like something is happening inside of them. Their eyes were glowing with excitement.

The girl in the front office looks up from her desk.

GIRL

Is there anything wrong?

KAREN

No. No. I'll get your order.

AL

Please let me help you . . . the box is quite heavy.

KAREN

All right.

They walk down the hall.

AL

How long have you been working here?

KAREN

Two years. It's just part time, three days a week.

She opens the door to the walk in cooler.

KAREN

This is your box of ribs.

AL

Thank you.

KAREN

Be sure to sign for them at the office.

AL

Look, I'm not trying to be forward, but could I invite you to dinner tomorrow night. I was coming this way anyway . . .

KAREN

(smiling)
No, I don't think so.

AL

Look I just want to be friends.

KAREN

I don't even know your name.

AL

Al. Al Strosaski. You like Mexican food?

Karen smiles and nods her head "yes."

AL

Then let's have dinner . . . I just want to be friends.

KAREN

Okay.

AL

I'll need your phone number.

Karen takes her pen and writes the number on the box of ribs.

AL

I'll see you about seven.

KAREN

(smiles)
That's fine.

The next evening Al was back in town and called Karen from a phone booth. The phone rings twice.

KAREN

Hello.

AL

Hi, this is Al. I'll need your address.

KAREN

Hi, Al how are you?

AL

Just fine, I'm sorry I'm a little late.

KAREN

Don't worry about it, I just got through getting dressed.

AL

Well I guess we're both on time then.

KAREN

(smiles)
I guess we are . . . my address is 1200 Fletcher Street. I live
on the north side of town.

AL

I'll see you in a few minutes.

He drives to her address and is now walking up her walk and rings her door bell.
Karen opens the door.

KAREN

My, you look very good in a three-piece suit.

AL

Thank you, you're looking very beautiful.

KAREN

Come in, I'll fix you a cup of tea.

The stereo is on.

AL

I believe that music is German.

KAREN

Yes, it is. Do you like it?

AL

Yes, it's a very beautiful piece.

Karen is in the kitchen fixing the cup of tea.

AL

Are you German?

KAREN

Yes, I am and you?

AL

I'm dutch. My folks both came from Holland.

KAREN

Do they live here in California?

AL

No they're both deceased.

KAREN

Oh, I'm sorry, I didn't mean to . . .

AL

That's all right, they passed on long ago.

KAREN

Here's your tea.

AL

Thank you.

KAREN

My folks still live in Germany. My father is half owner in a business.

AL

What kind of business does he have?

KAREN

Vonshrded & Hoffman, a carpet cleaning business. He does all right I guess.

AL

Would you like to go to any particular place for dinner?

KAREN

I was hoping you'd let me make your dinner here.

AL

I think that's great Karen. Let me help you.

KAREN

You can make the mash potatoes and that's all.

AL

I'll go for that.

———

As she makes dinner, they talk, have more tea and joke around. They get along really well. They've just finished their dinner now.

AL

That's the best beef stroganoff I have ever eaten.

KAREN

That's the best mash potatoes I have ever had.

They both smile.

KAREN

Let's go to the living room and change the music.

Karen also shows Al pictures of her family and it is now 1:00 in the morning. She puts the picture album in the dresser drawer. Al comes up behind her and puts his hands on her shoulders and turns her around. He slowly kisses her and they both embrace. His hands slowly go down to her ass and he's massaging her ass for about 10 seconds.

KAREN

No.

She stops him.

KAREN

I'm not that kind of a girl. I'm sorry if I disappoint you.

Al is breathing a little heavy.

AL

You don't disappoint me. I'm sorry.

KAREN

You'd better leave now if that's what you came for.

AL

That's not what I came for. I know you're not that kind of girl.

Al walks up to her and holds her by the shoulders.

AL

I'm sorry it won't happen again. It's getting late and I'd better go.

KAREN

I'm sorry.

AL

That's all right. I understand. I'm off in two days. Can I see you again?

KAREN

If you like.

Al kisses her on the cheek.

AL

I'll see you in two days.

He leaves.

Leach is on his way home from a movie that one of his friends had directed and wanted Leach to see how it had turned out. He stops at the Hungry Tiger for a drink. The lady that had been there two mornings ago was 3/4 down the bar. He goes in and sits next to her.

LEACH

Fancy meeting you here.

LADY

Hi Leach. What are you doing here so late?

LEACH

Just stopped by for a drink before I go home. I didn't get your name the other morning.

LADY

Sylvina. Sylvina Hudson.

LEACH

That's a very pretty name.

SYLVINA

I'm glad you like it Buck-o. You gonna buy me a drink?

LEACH

Sure. Samantha, give me a Bud and fill the lady's glass.

SYLVINA

I like your style, Leach. You act like you know what you're doing.

LEACH

I'm not acting.

SYLVINA

(as she looks him up and down)
You want to have a bite to eat with me?

LEACH

I think the kitchen is closed.

SYLVINA

I mean at my place.

LEACH

Sure, I'm a little hungry anyway. Where do you live?

SYLVINA

I'll show you.

They come to her car.

SYLVINA

You drive, Leach.

He opens the door to her Corvette and she shows her beautiful legs. She looks up at him and smiles. He smiles back and they drive off. Leach doesn't want to say much on the way to her house except that it was a nice night and asked what she had done that day. They pull in to her driveway and enter her house.

SYLVINA

Excuse me for a minute.

Sylvina goes to her bedroom.

Leach lights a cigarette and smokes it half way down. He never hears a sound from Sylvina. He looks at a picture.

LEACH

Are these your folks?

Sylvina does not answer and he looks at the bedroom door.

LEACH

Are you okay, Sylvina?

He walks to the door and sees her laying on the bed, on her back, her right leg was straight and her left leg was half way couked with her dress below her knee. The night light is on. He walks up to her and puts his hand on her stomach.

LEACH

Are you all right?

Sylvina reaches up and puts her arms around his neck and kisses him. Slowly he lays beside her. They roll over and then back again. They make love like it's their last day on Earth.

The next morning he doesn't wake her up. He calls a cab and picks up his car and goes home. He calls Eddy at work. A lady at the desk answers.

LADY DESK CLERK

Good morning, San Luis Bay Inn.

LEACH

Would you please page Eddy Moreno. He works in maintenance. I'l like to talk to him.

LADY DESK CLERK

Just one second.

She presses a button to the bar and the phone rings three times.

EDDY

Lounge, Eddy speaking.

LADDY DESK CLERK

Eddy you have a call on line three.

EDDY

Thank you.

28

He presses line three.

                    EDDY

Hello.

                    LEACH

Eddy, you old bastard, what have you been doing?

                    EDDY

Leach, what are you up to, where you at?

                    LEACH

I'm home. I just thought I'd call and see how you were doing.

                    EDDY

I'm doing fine. Working my ass off here at the hotel.

                    LEACH

Ha ha. Keep up the good work, maybe you'll get a raise.

                    EDDY

With the wages they pay here I don't know if I want to rough it anymore.

                    LEACH

Eddy, how the girls treating you? Have you found any angels yet?

                    EDDY

I found some ladies but no angels. I think they were discontinued in '39.

LEACH

Yeah, I guess they were. Eddy I was thinking maybe me, you and Al could get together Friday night and have a couple of drinks.

EDDY

That sounds great. Where should we meet?

LEACH

Over at Saydee's tavern, about seven. I'll call Al and let him know.

EDDY

Leach, I got to go. I'll see you Friday.

LEACH

Okay, Eddy. See ya.

Click. Clara has just walked in before Eddy hung up.

EDDY

Hello Clara, how are you this beautiful morning?

CLARA

Just fine, how are you?

EDDY

I'm doing all right, I guess. I'm almost done cleaning the bar. Can I pour you a drink?

CLARA

(smiles)
Heavens no, I don't drink.

EDDY

You live around here, Clara?

CLARA

Yes, I live at 310 Front. St. I've been there about six months.

EDDY

Where did you come from?

CLARA

Arizona. Haydrin, Arizona. It's just a little town. Where are you from Eddy?

EDDY

Los Angeles. I was born and raised there.

CLARA

I've never been there. Is it a nice town?

EDDY

It's all right if you have friends and know where to go. Other than that, it's dog eat dog.

Clara just stares at him for a few seconds then turns her head toward the window.

CLARA

Do you go to the beach often?

EDDY

Yes, I do. I like walking on the beach.

CLARA

So do I.

EDDY

Maybe someday we can walk on the beach together.

CLARA

(looks at him)
Maybe someday. I'd better get back to work before Pea
finds me loafing. I'll see you.

EDDY

Have a good day, Clara.

The day goes by fairly fast for Eddy. He is now having a beer at a local beer bar
and cannot help overhearing a
    A couple is arguing in the corner booth.

Lady: "I don't care what you say, Matt, I'm not going back to you."
Man: "You're being very childish, aren't you?"
Lady: "I don't think so; I caught you with that bitch three times now and
          each time you said you weren't going to see her anymore."

    Eddy finishes his beer and goes to see Doris. He pulls up in front of her
house and goes to the door and knocks. A lady opens the door and says, "Yes,
may I help you?"

Eddy: "I'm looking for Doris. Is she here?"
Lady: "She doesn't live here anymore."
Eddy: "Do you know where she went to?"
Lady: "I have no idea. When I moved in I heard the lady that lived here
          moved out of town."
Eddy: "Well . . . thank you very much."

    The lady just smiles and Eddy leaves.
    Eddy is driving on the freeway and suddenly remembers Clara's address, ???,
310 Front Street, all right and drives to a villa about four miles away and parks

his pickup in front of her house and knocks on the door. Clara opens the door, smiles and says, "What are you doing here?:

Eddy: "I just thought I'd come by and say hello."
Clara: "This is a surprise."
Eddy: "I hope you weren't busy."
Clara: "No. I just got through with my sewing.
Eddy: "Aren't you going to ask me in?"

Clara phased for a couple of seconds. "I usually don't allow men in my apartment."

Eddy: "Well . . . I'm not a nut. I'm not going to bite you."

Clara phased for a moment. "Well, I guess you're all right. Come in."

Eddy: "Thank you . . . It's a nice little place you have here."
Clara: "I love it; it's very peaceful here."

Eddy just smiles and kinds of nods his head.

Clara: "Would you like some coffee? I have a fresh pot."
Eddy: "Yes I would. Thank—ou."
Clara: "Have a seat. I'll be one minute."

Eddy sits down and looks around. "You like working at the hotel?"

Clara: "Yes, I do. I wish I was more than just a maid. Do you take sugar in your coffe?"
Eddy: "Two, please. Maids are just as important as a top executive. You can't function without them."
Clara: "It's nice of you to say that. Do you like working there so far?"
Eddy: "It's all right. It's a lot different than what I was doing."
Clara: "What kind of work were you doing in Los Angeles?"
Eddy: "I, ah . . . was working for a movie studio.
Clara: "Really? That must have been exciting work."
Eddy: "I liked it a lot. It pays real good."
Clara: "What happened? Why did you leave?"
Eddy: "I got tired of it. I wanted to go to a place like this—no smog, no traffic jams, not nuts."
Clara: "Then it's quite a change for you."

Eddy:	"A very big change, yes."
Clara:	"Do you plan to stay long in this area?"
Eddy:	"Yes, I plan to get married and raise a couple of kids in this area."
Clara:	"What nice thoughts you have."
Eddy:	"Would you like to go out for a sandwich or a pizza?"
Clara:	"I . . . don't think so. I'm rather tired and I want to get some rest tonight. It's getting late."
Eddy:	"Well, maybe tomorrow . . . I'll bring you home early."
Clara:	"Well . . . alright."
Eddy:	"I'll pick you up at six o'clock tomorrow. Goodnight."
Clara:	"Goodnight."

Eddy picks up Clara for dinner the next night and takes her to a nice restaurant. They have an excellent dinner and after dinner they talk and talk and talk and then go window shopping, holding hands and making jokes and laughing. The following night he takes her out to dinner and to a movie and they're now on their way to Clara's house.

Clara:	"I've been having a wonderful time, Eddy. I want to thank you."
Eddy:	"I've been having a great time, too, Clara. I want to thank you for making me feel ten feet tall."

Clara smiles. "Oh come on, Eddy."

Eddy:	"No, I'm serious. I haven't felt this way for a long time. I also think you're a very beautiful lady." He pulls in front of her house. "Let me get that door for you."

They walk to her front door and she gets her key from her purse. Eddy takes it from her hand and opens the door and they both walk in. He takes her by the hand and slowly draws her toward him. He kisses her and they both embrace. They hold each other very tightly. His hands go down to her ass.

Clara:	"No, Eddy, no."
Eddy:	"What's wrong?"
Clara:	"I don't want to be treated like a tramp."
Eddy:	"I didn't mean any harm."
Clara:	"I don't think it's right to have sex unless you're married."
Eddy:	"Well, I—I wasn't trying to be smart."
Clara:	"I'm a virgin."

Eddy: "A virg ... well ... there's nothing wrong with that. I didn't mean to upset you."
Clara: "That's all right."
Eddy: "Sit down, Clara, please. I want to talk to you." She sits down on the couch. He says, "I want to say something to you and I want you to listen. You're the best thing that's ever happened to me. I love you and I want you to be my wife."
Clara: "But you *don't know me*."
Eddy: "All I know is that you're everything that's good."

Clara stares at Eddy with such innocent eyes and barely smiles.

Eddy: "I love you more than my life."
Clara: "Eddy, you don't know what you're saying."
Eddy: "I assure you I do, Clara. Believe me ... I do."
Clara: "Let's talk about this some other time. Please, it's getting late."
Eddy: "Sure, that's fine. I'll see you tomorrow. Okay?"

Clara just smiles and nods her head yes. Eddy kisses her gently and says goodnight and leaves.

THE NEXT DAY

Leach has been working about three hours and asks Joanne, a waitress, "Where's Sandy, Joanne?"

Joanne: "Oh, I'm sorry, I thought you knew."
Leach: "Knew what?"
Joanne: "Sandy's mom. She died."
Leach: "Died?"
Joanne: "Last night about seven. She won't be back until after the burial."
Leach: "That's too bad. I didn't know."
Joanne: "I need a Bud and a separator."

Leach mixes a separator and gets a Bud. "That'll be $4.50."
The afternoon goes by quickly and soon he is punching the time clock. He is driving through town when he sees Sandy through a restaurant window. He parks his car and goes to the restaurant and walks in.

Leach: "Sandy, I heard about your mom. I'm very sorry."

Sandy: "Thank you, Leach. I appreciate your being concerned. Sit down. I want to introduce you to my sister, Bell. Bell, this is Leach, a friend of mine."

Bell: "It's a pleasure to meet you, Leach."

Leach: "The pleasure's all mine, Bell. Like I said, I'm sorry about your mom. I'd like to come to the funeral if I may.

Sandy: "Of course, Leach. You're very welcome."

Leach: "Is there anything I can do for any of you?"

Bell: "No thanks, Leach. We've got it pretty much under control."

Leach: "You both seem to be taking it pretty good."

Sandy: "We knew she was dying but we didn't know when."

Leach: "Well, when the good Lord calls you I guess He calls you for a reason."

Leach goes to the funeral and plays a big part in comforting Sandy and Bell. It's now late afternoon and Leach has just driven the girls to their apartment from the funeral.

Leach: "I won't be coming in, girls. I think it's best if you two were alone to talk."

Bell: "You're welcome to come in, Leach."

Leach: "I know, Bell. Thanks, but it's best this way."

As the girls are walking to their apartment Leach says, "Bell?" Bell comes back to the car.

Leach: "Look, ahh . . . is it all right to drop in from time to time to see how you're doing?"

Bell: "I wish you would, Leach."

Leach: "Thank you, Bell. I'll see you."

Al has just picked up Karen and they're on their way to town. They go to a park and walk around. He pushes her on the swing. They have a lot of fun and act like two lovebirds. They are walking through the park smiling and joking when he picks her up in his arms and swirls her around. He falls to ground with her still in his arms and kisses her.

Al: "I love you, Karen."

Karen: "I think a lot of you, Al."

Al kisses her on the neck.

Karen: "Al, people are looking."

Al: "Good, I want the world to know I'm in love with you."
Karen: "Ha-ha-ha. Al, you're crazy."
Al: "Over you, my love. Tonight we're going dancing after we have
            dinner."
Karen: "Where are you taking me?"
Al: "Some place that's quiet with soft music."

That night Al takes her to a fine restaurant, Delmonico's, ands they have just finished their dinner.

Al: "That dinner was very well prepared."
Karen: "It was very good. I enjoyed it."
Al: "Karen, you look very pretty with the light shining on you the way
            it is."

Karen smiles. "Thank you, Al, you're very kind."

Al: ""Karen, I have something for you. I hope you like it."
Karen: "Oh, what is it?"
Al: "Close your eyes and don't open them till I say so."

Karen closes her eyes. Al reaches inside his suit coat pocket and retrieves a small blue box with an engagement ring and wedding band. He opens the box.

Al: "Open your eyes, Karen."

Karen opens her eyes and sees the rings. Her eyes are filled with joy.

Karen: "Al, how could you? I mean . . . huh . . . they're beautiful."
Al: "You like them?"

"They're gorgeous," Karen says, clutching them to her breast.

Al: "I want you to be my wife, Karen."

Karen just stares at Al with a big smile. Slowly taking the smile off her face, she says, "Al, we just met. How could you be sure?"

Al: "Ever since I was a little kid I knew when I saw the woman I wanted
            to marry, I would feel a special way." He reaches for her hand. "I now
            have that special feeling."

Karen: "Al, I don't know what to say."
Al: "Say you'll be my wife."
Karen: "At least let me think it over."
Al: "Sure, I understand . . . Would you like to dance?"
Karen: "I'd love to, Al."

They dance the night away till about 1:30. The band quits playing at that time.

Karen: "I had a wonderful time, Al."
Al: "I had a great time, too, Karen. I can't believe this is happening to me."

Karen puts her head on his shoulder. "I'm so tired, Al. Will you please take me home?"

Al: "Yes, of course.

The next evening about 6:30 Al arrives at Sadie's Tavern and sits at the bar.

Al: "Could I have a bottle of Budweiser, please?"
Barmaid: "Would you like a cold glass.?"
Al: "Sure, I'll take a glass. (Pause) This is not one of your busier days, is it?"
Barmaid: "About seven everybody starts coming in. That's one dollar, please."

Leach and Eddy enter the bar at the same time.

Al: "Hey Eddy, Leach, good to see you guys again. Long time no see."
Leach: "How you been, Al?"
Al: "Good, good."
Eddy: "You're gaining a little weight, huh, Al?"
Al: "No way. Gimme a break, Eddy. Lady, two more Buds, please."
Leach: "Hell, Al's buying. He must be makin' a lot of money."
Al: "Ha, ha, ha. I'm making five dollars an hour and that's a bitch."
Eddy: "That ain't shit. I'm making four dollars."
Al: "This situation is too much. Ha, ha. I'll be glad when this is over. No, not really. I met a little angel."
Leach: "You did? So did I."
Eddy: "I met an angel myself."

Al:	"I'm going to marry her."
Eddy:	"Have you asked her?"
Al:	"Yes. She wants to think it over, but I know she's gonna say yes. I just know she is. Are you gonna ask yours to married, Leach?"
Leach:	"Well, it's a little early to tell but she's definitely the girl I want to marry. There's a strong attraction between us. Yes, Goddamnit, as soon as I see her I'm gonna ask her to get married."
Eddy:	"Clara is thinking it over, too . . . Yes, she's going to marry me, I know she will. Things are looking great. I think we're all going back to L.A. with three little angels. I guess we can all say goodbye to the bachelor's life pretty quick."
Al:	"That really sounds fantastic. Hey, I've got an idea. Let's get the girls together so we can all meet each other and have dinner somewhere."
Leach:	"When shall we do this?"
Al:	"As soon as possible."
Eddy:	"As soon as we get ready let's call Leach and we'll go from there."
Leach:	"Good enough. Lady, three more Buds, please. All right, which one of you wants to lose a game of pool?"
Eddy:	"Go ahead, Al, show him how this game is played.
Leach:	"Shit, Al, I don't even know how to shoot."
Al:	"Huh, this is going to be duck soup."

Eddy puts a quarter on the table to challenge the next game."

Al:	"Pay attention, Leach, you might not get a shot."
Leach:	"Shoot your best, Al."

Al breaks. The seven and eleven balls go into two different pockets. He shoots again and makes another; again he shoots and again he makes his shot. He takes careful aim at a bank shot and misses.

Leach:	"Al, you might as well hang up your cue . . ." At that moment two men enter the establishment and sit at the bar to drink beer. " . . . 'cause you ain't getting any more shots."
Al:	"You can win if you make 'em all and don't miss a shot. You miss one shot and it's my show."

Leach just smiles; taking his time, he makes his shot. The two men at the bar keep looking over their shoulders, talking to each other in a low tone. Leach takes his time, makes nine consecutive shots, making each shot count. He is now aiming at his last ball before he shoots the eight ball. He shoots and makes his shot, scratching the cue ball on the side pocket.

Leach: "Goddamnit."
Al: "Well, Leach, comes a time in a man's life when it's necessary to shoot all the engineers to get the job done himself. Stand by."

Al calls his pocket and takes careful aim at the eight ball. Just before he shoots the big construction man drops his hard hat helmet, causing Al to miss.

Al: "Shit!"

The big construction man picks his helmet up off the floor and says, "I'm sorry. I didn't do that on purpose."
Al just looks at him like he wants to bust him in the mouth. "He did it on purpose, Eddy."

Eddy: "Forget it, Al, it was just an accident."

The two men at the bar laugh.

Leach: "Corner pocket, Al . . . I guess you were right about those engineers."

Leach shoots the eight ball in the corner. The cue ball hits the rail, comes all the way back and scratches in the corner pocket."

Eddy: "Tough break, Leach, but you shoot a hell of a game."

The big construction man gets up and says, "I'll play the winner."

Eddy: "I'm playing the next game."

The big man says, "Who said so?"

Eddy: "I got my quarter on the table for the next challenge."
Big Man: "You play the next one."
Eddy: "I'm playing this one."

The big man's 275 pounds outweigh Eddy by 75 pounds. Eddy is stocky and strong, too. The big man swings. Eddy ducks and hits the big man with a right between the mouth and the nose. The concussion of the blow backs the big man a step back. Faster than a heartbeat the big man charges Eddy and grabs Eddy in bear hug, slamming him against the wall. At the same time some beer bottles on display on a shelf fall. The big man holds Eddy high, applying painful pressure to Eddy's back. Eddy hits the man with a left and then a right. The man applies more pressure to Eddy's back. The pain is so strong Eddy grinds his teeth and his head is leaning far back. Eddy sees a beer mug on the shelf next to his head. Eddy grabs the mug and hits the man twice on the forehead, breaking the mug on the second hit. The big man's knees start to buckle. Eddy hits the man with his elbow. The man falls, dropping Eddy to the floor. The big man is out cold. Eddy reaches for the top of the pool table, struggling to get up. The other man at the bar stands up, walking toward Eddy. Leach steps in front of him and says, "Let's call it a draw."

The man stops and stares at Leach with hateful eyes, then turns to the big man on the floor to help him up. Leach walks over to Eddy and says, "Let me help you, Eddy."

Al also helps him up, saying, "You okay, Eddy?"

Eddy: "Yeh, unh . . . oh shit," reaching for the small of his back.
Al: "What's wrong?"
Eddy: "My back, my fuckin' back. I think it's broken."
Leach: "Let's get you out of here. You'll be alright."
Eddy: "That guy . . . he'd make a hell of a chiropractor, huh."

The next day Leach is about to get off work when his manager, Lorada, says, "Leach, Barbara is going to be late for work. Would you mind working till about nine? I hope you haven't anything planned."

Leach: "No, I haven't anything planned. Sure, I can work till nine."
Lorada: "Are you sure, Leach?"
Leach: "I'm positive, Lorada. Don't worry about it."
Lorada: "Thanks, Leach. I knew I could count on you."

As she walks away Leach says, "Lorada, you sure have a nice ass."

Lorada: "Leach, is that all you have on your mind?"

Leach just looks at her with a smile and shakes his head yes. Lorada exits just shaking her head. That night time goes by real fast. Leach looks at the clock and says, "Wow, it's nine o'clock."

Lady at bar: "It's amazing how fast time goes by when you're busy."

Leach: "Well, I had me quite a rush there." Picking up the ladys glass, "Would
            you like another glass of white wine?"
Lady: "Yes, please . . . I wonder what time that jerk is going to pick me up."
Leach: "Pardon me, I didn't hear you."
Lady: "Nothing, nothing. I'm just talking to myself."

Leach hands her a glass of wine and picks up two dollars and fifty cents.
"Thank you."
    At that time three guys and Karen come in laughing and joking and kissing
her and now and then sliding their hands down her ass. They sit down on the
other end of the bar on a couch and lounge chair. One man says, "Bartender, two
Budweisers, one Heineken and one gin and tonic."

Leach: "Very good, sir."

Leach makes the gin and tonic and gets the beers. "Seven fifty, sir."
The man gives him a ten and says, "Keep the change."

Leach: "Thank you, sir."

He keeps serving drinks to customers. Twenty minutes later Karen and her
friends order another round and twenty minutes later they order another round.
Karen is feeling good by now. She is sitting on the couch and her dress is about
eight inches above her knees. One of the men comes to the bar for more drinks.

Leach: "Four more of the same, sir?"
Man: "Yes, please."

Leach gets the three beers and starts to mix the gin and tonic. Leach looks
at Karen's beautiful legs and says to the man, "Looks like a real nice girl."
    The man looks at Leach, then at Karen. He smiles and looks back at Leach
and says, "She is nice . . . *EXCELLENT*."

Leach: "Seven fifty, sir."

The barmaid shows up.

Leach: "Well, it's about time, beautiful."
Barmaid: "I'm sorry, Leach. I can't explain now."
Leach: "That's all right, sweetheart. I'll interrogate you later. I've got to go
            now. I'm having supper with a very special lady. Ciao." He exits.

Karen is having the time of her life. One man puts his hand on her thigh, kisses her and says, "Let's go."

Al has been waiting all this time in front of Karen's house. He looks at his watch; it is 1:30. He lights a cigarette, looks up the street. There is no traffic. He looks down the street and there's also no traffic. He walks to his car and takes off back home. He stops at the motel to have a drink. There is a good crowd threre. He is worried about Karen. It flashes through his mind about the good times they had together. Time goes by. He's at the end of his fourth beer when one of the cooks comes by.

Cook: "Al, how you doing?"
Al: "Huh? Hey, how's it going? You just get off work?"
Cook: "Yeah, about thirty minutes ago. Let me buy you a beer. Jerry, two beers. So what's new?"

Al spots a girl that resembles Karen across the bar in a booth, talking to some guys.

Al: "Excuse me a second, I think I know this lady."

He walks slowly across the bar floor and the dance floor since there is a good crowd and taps her on the shoulder. The lady turns and says, "Yes?" The guy with the lady looks at Al.

Al: "I'm sorry, I thought you were someone I knew."

The lady just smiles.

Al: "I'm sorry." He makes his way back to the bar.
Cook: "Who was that?"
Al: "I thought it was someone I knew."

At that time a girl comes by.

Cook: "Hey, Lina, where you going?"
Lina: "I'm going home. That creep I was with pissed me off."
Cook: "Wait, I'll take you home. Al, I'll see you later."
Al: "Yeah, I'll see you tomorrow.

The next day Al calls Karen early in the morning about seven. Ring, ring, ring, ring, ring, ring, ring.

Karen:	"Hello?"
Al:	"Hi. I couldn't find you last night."
Karen:	"Al, what time is it?"
Al:	"Seven-o-five."
Karen:	"What's wrong? Why are you calling so early?"
Al:	"I just wanted to know if you were alright. I was worried about you."
Karen:	"Yes, I'm alright. I went for a ride last night. I wanted to think things over."
Al:	"Listen, they're breaking in a new cook tonight and tomorrow I'm off. I'll pick you up for dinner tonight."
Karen:	"Oh, Al, I'm so tired."
Al:	"Come on, I'll take you back home early. I want you to meet a friend of mine. I'll have you home before nine. Okay?"
Karen:	"Oh, Al . . ."
Al:	"Come on, don't be a lazy lady."
Karen:	"If you promise to bring me home by nine."
Al:	"I'll have you home particularly early. I'll pick you up about four."
Karen:	"I'll be ready."
Al:	"I love you, Karen."
Karen:	"I'll see you later, Al."
Al:	"Bye."
Karen:	"Bye."

Karen hangs up the phone and says, "Oh my God, I'll never have another drink as long as I live."

Al has already picked up Karen and is driving down the freeway.

Al:	"Well, it sounds like you had a good ride last night. What time did you get home?"
Karen:	"About two o'clock. I just needed time to think, Al."
Al:	"I understand, Karen. I want you to meet a friend of mine. He's a good guy. You're going to like him."
Karen:	"What's his name?"
Al:	"Eddy, Eddy Moreno. He works for the San Luis Bay Inn in Avila. He's kinda like a bum. He lives in his camper."
Karen:	"In his camper . . . in a camper? You mean in a camper camper?"
Al:	"Yes, ha, ha, ha. I mean a camper camper. He's got everything in there, a bed, a stove, ice box, closet. You name it, he's got it.
Karen:	"God, I don't know if I want to meet your friend. Ha, ha. I'm just kidding."

They drive down the freeway about another mile and take the first Pismo off ramp.

Karen: "I haven't been in this town for about three years."
Al: "You know anyone here?"
Karen: "No, I just used to visit the town once in a while."
Al: "There's Eddy's truck. Now he said he meet us here at this Filipino restaurant."

Al parks in front of the restaurant. Before Al gets out of thecar he tells Karen, "Just one second. I'll get that door for you."

He gets out and goes around the front of the car and opens her door . . . She enteres the restaurant first. The screen door closes behind them.

Al: "Eddy, how's it going?"
Eddy: (as they shake hands) "Real good, Al, real good."
Al: "Eddy, this is Karen. Karen, this is Eddy, my friend I was telling you about."
Karen: "I'm pleased to meet you, Eddy."
Eddy: "I'm certainly pleased to meet you. Al was right, you know."
Karen: "Ah . . ."
Al: "You are a very beautiful woman."

Karen smiles and says, "Thank you."

Al: "Well, let's sit down and have something to eat. Okay?"
Karen: "Well, I never had Filipino food before."
Eddy: "Order sarsado and you won't be sorry."
Karen: "What is it?"
Eddy: "Vegetables with chunks of beef."
Al: That sounds reall good. I think I'll try that. What do you think, Karen?"
Karen: "Sure, I'll give it a try."
Al: "What are you going to have, Eddy?"
Eddy: "Sarsado. I ordered about ten seconds before you two walked in. Let me tell Nanay to put two more orders on."

Eddy goes to the kitchen door. "Nanay, two more sarsados for my friends."

Nanay: "Okay, Eddy, okay."

Eddy comes back to the table and sits down.

Karen: "This sure is a small restaurant."
Eddy: "I come here almost every day. I like it. It's real home cooking."

Karen smiles.

Eddy: "I'm going to get me a Budweiser. Would you like one, Karen?"
Karen: "No thank you. I don't drink."
Nanay: "Here we are. Three sarsados, one for you and one for you. Who does this other one go to?

Eddy raises his head looks at Nanay.

Nanay: "Ha, ha, ha. I knew I would shake you up, Eddy."
Eddy: "Nanay, you always treat me mean."
Nanay: "How do American girls say? You love it, you love it." Everybody laughs. "You eat now. I go to the kitchen."
Eddy: "Nanay, two Buds, please."
Nanay: "Ahh . . ."
Karen: "This food looks terrific."
Al: "It smells good, too."
Eddy: "Sure does. What kind of work do you do, Karen?"
Karen: "I work for a wholesale meat company three days a week."
Eddy: "You like it?"
Karen: "Not really. I'd rather be in Beverly Hills as a big secretary in a high rise building. Ha, ha. Not really."
Eddy: "Might be you'll get your chance."
Karen: "Ha, fat chance."

They eat their dinner and talk about everything and anything. Thirty minutes have passed.

Nanay: "More beer, Eddy?"
Eddie: "No, I think that's it for me. How about you, Al?"
Al: "I've had it. Would you like something else, Karen?"
Karen: "No thank you, Al. I'm alright."
Eddy: "Nanay, bring me the check."
Al: "I've got it, Eddy."
Eddy: "No, you don't."
Al: "I'll flip you for it."

Eddy: "Wrong again."
Nanay: "Here you go, Eddy."
Eddy: "Ha, huh . . . here, Nanay, you keep the change."
Nanay: "Oh, Eddy, thank you. I will not tease you again. Ha, ha."
Eddy: "Well, I love you, Nanay."
Al: "Well, I guess I'll be getting you home, Karen. You wanted to be home by nine."
Karen: "Yes, please, Al. I'm very tired."
Eddy: "Well, Karen, it was very nice to have met you and I'm sure we'll see each other again."
Karen: "The pleasure was all mine, Eddy. I'm sure we will."
Al: "We'll see you, Eddy. You take care. Come up and visit me some time."
Eddy: "I will. I've been very busy but I will."

All and Karen leave the restaurant and drive away. Eddy is watching them through the window. He continues to stare out the window for about thirty seconds, then turns around and says to Nanay, "Goodnight, Nanay, I'll see you tomorrow."

Nanay: "Goodnight, Eddy, goodnight."

Eddy drives to Avila to see Clara. He arrives at her house in about fifteen minutes. He knocks on her door. Clara is doing her nails at the time she hears a knock on her door again.

Clara: "Just a minute." She puts the bottle of lacquer on the table and goes to the door and opens it.
Eddy: "Hello, Clara."
Clara: "Hi."
Eddy: "Could I come in?"
Clara: "Of course, come in. I'm doing my nails. You don't mind, do you?"
Eddy: "Not at all. I just thought I'd come by and see if you would like to go for a ride."
Clara: "I'll just finish my nails, Eddy, and I'm going to bed. I don't feel good at all."
Eddy: "Well, I'll just visit for a while."
Clara: "*Eddy, please*, I'm trying to be nice . . .

Eddy is amazed by her behavior. "I'm sorry, I . . . I have to go anyway. I'll see you tomorrow, okay?"

Clara:	"I'm sorry, Eddy, but I'm not feeling well."
Eddy:	"That's all right. I understand. I'll see you tomorrow."
Eddy:	"Good night."
Clara:	"Good night, Eddy."

Eddy leaves and drives away along the waterfront town. He stops at the corner grocery store to get a beer and is on his way again. He drives into San Luis and stops at Sadie's. He's just finished his first beer.

Eddy:	"Could I have another beer, please?"
Barmaid:	"Sure."

A lady walks up to Eddy.

Eddy:	"Hi . . . how you doing?"
Lady:	"Fine. I've never seen you here before."
Eddy:	"Been here most of the summer. This is my second time here at Sadie's. You come here a lot, do you?"
Lady:	"Yes, I'm a regular. What's your name?"
Eddy:	"Eddy Moreno. What's yours?"
Lady:	"Susan."
Eddy:	"Susan, could I buy you a drink?"
Susan:	"Sure, I'd like one. Thank you."

Eddy signals the barmaid. The barmaid comes and asks Susan, "The usual, Susan?"

Susan:	"Yes, please . . . Your name sure sounds familiar."

Eddy just looks at her.

Susan:	"I've heard it or read it somewhere or some place.
Eddy:	"Never been there."
Susan:	"What's that?"
Eddy:	"I'm just kidding. Let's play pool. You want to? I'll show you a couple of good shots."
Susan:	"All right. But I'll have to warn you I'm the best shot in town."
Eddy:	"That's good. I like competition."

They play about ten games, laughing and hugging each other. Then they sit down and talk and drink for about an hour.

Eddy: "Well, shit. Let's go for a ride, Susan."
Susan: "Where to?"
Eddy: "Anywhere. Let's get some fresh air. It's too smokey in here."
Susan: "Let's go."

They leave the bar and drive northwest of Morrow Bay.

Eddy: "This sure is pretty country."
Susan: "I like it. I was born and raised here. Raised my children here. I wouldn't leave for the world."
Eddy: "It's the best I've seen, and I've been all over the world."
Susan: "What kind of work do you do, Eddy?"
Eddy: "I'm a writer. I write stories for the movies."
Susan: "Oh yeah? Well, how about writing about me in your next movie?"
Eddy: "You got it. I'll write you in my next story."
Susan: "Ha-ha-ha. You're crazy, but I like you anyway." She kisses him on the cheek.

Eddy pulls over by some pine trees by the ocean.

Susan: "Why are you stopping?"
Eddy: "I have some beer in my ice chest in the back. Want one?"
Susan: "Sure."
Eddy: "Come on. I'll show you my camper."

They get out of the truck and go to the back. He unlocks the door and opens it.

Eddy: "Step into my parlor."
Susan: (as she climbs into the camper) "You're drunk."
Eddy: "No, I'm not. Hiccup!"

He also enters the camper and turns the light switch on.

Eddy: "This is my home away from home."
Susan: "I don't believe you have another home. I think this is lock, stock and barrel."
Eddy: "I wouldn't jive a beautiful woman like you."

They look at each other for a few seconds, then kiss, then embrace. The camper looks nice with the ocean in the background. Then the lights go out.

Five hours later it's the beginning of dawn. The camper still looks good against the ocean and the light of day creeping up. Everything is silent. Then you can hear Susan addressing Eddy.

Susan: "Eddy, get up. I'll be late for work." She shakes him by the shoulder. "Wake up, wake up. I've got to get to work."
Eddy: "Huh? Ah . . ."
Susan: "I'm going to be late for work if you don't get me home right away. Get up."

Eddy starts to get up and hits his head on the of the cab-over bed. "Ouch!" They're on their way back and approaching San Luis.

Eddy: "Don't worry. I'm going to get you to work on time."
Susan: "Are you going to work?"
Eddy: "Nah." Rubbing his face he says, "I've got a bad hangover. I think I'll go to the beach and just kick back."
Susan: "Go down this street three block, then turn left."

Eddy lights a cigarette and starts to turn right.

Susan: "No, no. Left. You have to turn left."

Eddy turns left.

Susan: "It's the fourth house on the right."
Eddy: "You're a pain in the ass." He looks at her and smiles. "But I love you."
Susan: "Stop here." She gets out of the truck. "I'll see you," she says and starts running up the driveway.
Eddy: "Hey, I'll see you."

He just stares at the house for a second or two and then drives away. He goes to a nearby coffee shop to have breakfast.

Waitress: "Coffee, sir?"
Eddy: "Yes, please."

The waitress goes to get the coffee pot and comes back.

Eddy: "I guess I'll have bacon and eggs, no potatoes. I'll have my eggs scrambled."

Waitress: "How many eggs?"
Eddy: "Half a dozen." The waitress stops writing and looks at Eddy who
          says, "What's wrong."
Waitress: "Nothing. I'm sorry."

After breakfast Eddy thinks he'll go to Avila to see Clara before she goes to work. He comes upon the town of Avila. It's so peaceful and the ocean is so calm. He parks his car about half a block from Clara's apartment, walks to her door and knocks. There is no answer. He walks to his pickup admiring the beach. There is hardly anyone on the beach, since it's 7:30 in the morning. He stops in front of his truck and lights a cigarette. He takes a couple of puffs from his cigarette and turns around slowly toward Clara's apartment. He sees a new Corvette approaching Clara's apartment but doesn't pay much attention at the moment. Then he slowly does a double take and focuses on the passenger side of the car. There is Clara. Some guy is bringing her home from a one night stand.

Eddy: "Clara." He stares in disbelief for a split second. He knows his dream
          of getting married to her are shattered.
Eddy: "Clara." The gentleman with her gets out of the car and opens her
          door and walks her to the door. Eddy just stands in shock. Then he
          walks to her door and knocks. When she doesn't answer her door he
          opens the door and she is just getting through changing into her work
          clothes. She looks at him and says in an angry voice, "*Well? Well?*"

Eddy stares at her for a couple of seconds and says, "I'll walk you to work." He closes the door. It is about a quarter to eight and Clara starts work at eight. He waits about one minute and she comes out to go to work, walking faster than usual. He walks beside her, not saying anything for about thirty seconds.

Eddy: "How many times have you spent the night with Him?"
Clara: "I didn't spend the night with him. He picked me up this morning
          and we went to breakfast."
Eddy: "You put high heels and a fancy dress on to have breakfast? Come
          on, Clara, I'm not an idiot."

Clara doesn't say anything, just keeps walking with a worried look on her face.

Eddy: "Answer me, Goddamn it! I'm talking to you!"
Clara: "Leave me alone."
Eddy: "I want to talk to you, Clara. When you get off work I want to talk
          to you."

Clara: "No. I don't want to talk to you. Leave me alone."

She starts running toward the hotel where she works, and Eddy does not pursue her. He stops and watches her till she reaches the driveway of the hotel, then starts back to his truck. A cold sweat comes over him by the time he gets back to his truck and he is exhausted. He drives to a nearby campground about ten miles away, parks and lies on his bed but the cold sweat just gets worse. He lies in bed all day with the cold sweat.

That same evening Al is having a beer at the motel in and talking to a waitress named Sonya.

Sonya: "Are you having supper here, Al?"
Al: "No, I'm having dinner at my girl's house."
Sonya: "Hey, I heard you talking about her before. This is getting pretty serious . . . mmm."
Al: "Well, I'm hoping to get married to her."
Sonya: "Al, congratulations! I'm so happy for you. When is the big day?"
Al: "Well, I won't know until tomorrow. I'm asking her tonight."
Sonya: "Al, I'm dancing at your wedding. Let's drink a toast." She grabs his glass of beer. "To you and your beautiful bride." She drinks the full tall mug of beer and puts the mug down on the bar.
Sonya: "I'll see you later. I've got to get to work."

Al just stares at her as she walks away.

Al pulls up in front of Karen's house. He goes to her door and knocks and knocks but to no avail. She is gone again. He goes to his car and looks back at her house, kind of biting his bottom lip in a worried manner. He thinks he will drive to Morrow Bay and visit Leach. When he gets to the bar where Leach works Leach is sitting at the bar having a drink.

Al: "Leach, how ya doing?"
Leach: "Al, what are you doing here?"
Al: "Just stopped by for a drink."
Leach: "That's good. I'm glad to see you.

The bar mad comes and Al says, "Scotch and soda."

Leach: "Seen Eddy?"
Al: "Yeh, we had dinner with the girls the other night."
Leach: "Where's your girl?"

Al: "I don't know. She wasn't home. I was supposed to take her out tonight."

Leach: "Me and my girl are going out to dinner tonight. Why don't you come along with us?"

Al: "I don't think so, Leach. I think I'm just going to hang around here tonight."

Leach: "Whatever you say, pal. Hey, there's a lot of nice ladies that come in here. You won't have any trouble picking one up."

Al: "Well, it's good to know. Now I'm going to stay. You want another drink?"

Leach: "No, I've got to pick up my girl. You sure you wont join us?"

Al: "I'm sure."

Leach: "Hey, give me a call during the week, let me know what's happening."

Al: "O.K."

Leach: "Take it easy." He exits.

Al orders another drink goes to the restroom. At that time Karen and two guys walk in laughing and joking and go all the way to the end of the bar and sit on the corner couch just around the bar, out of Al's view from where he would be sitting. Al comes back and continues to drink his drink. The band starts to play music. Some couples get up and dance. Al isn't really in a dancing mood. He has Karen on his mind. Two beautiful ladies come in and go all the way to the back of the bar to get a seat. Al decides to go talk to them. Just before he reaches their table he looks at where Karen and her friends are sitting. He stops in his tracks. One guy puts his arm around her and kisses her.

In a low voice Al says, "What's going on here?"

He walks to their table. The guy has just finished kissing her. Karen is surprised to see Al.

Karen: "Al, what are you doing here?"

Al looks surprised and sad at the same time and says, "What's the meaning of this?"

Karen: (pulling her dress down a little) "Al, these are some friends of mine."

Al: "Is this where you spend your fucking time when I I can't find you?"

One guy gets up and puts his hand on on Al's shoulder.

Guy: "Just a minute, pal."

Al slugs the man and knocks him halfway over the couch. Karen screams and the other man gets up. Karen gets up and stands between Al and the other man.

Karen: "Al, please! You're making a scene." She holds his wrist. "Please sit down."

Al jerks his hand back in anger. The band has stopped playing and the people are staring. Al storms out of the bar. Karen chases him almost to the front door saying, "Al, wait. You don't understand." Then she stopped. "Al?"

Al drove away, furious, to the waterfront, parked the car and walked aimlessly. Finally he came to the end of this jetty looking across the bay, wondering how this happened.

Al: "This is not true." (putting his fist up to his lips) "It can't be true."

Staring at the lights of the city in a thoughtless mind, five hours pass before he gets up from a rock he had been sitting on goes to his car. He drives back to Karen's house. The lights are on. He knocks at her door . . . he knocks again . . . and again.

Karen opens the door, says, "I don't want to talk to you," and starts to close the door.

Al blocks the door with his foot and grabs the doorknob. "Karen, I have to talk to you, please."

Karen: "No."
Al: "I have to talk to you, Karen." Pushing the door open he says in a loud voice, "Can't you see I'm going crazy?" He slams the door shut.

She had been getting ready for bed and has on a long silk see-through nightgown. She backs into the front room. There is a silence.

Al: "Why didn't you tell me?"

Karen doesn't answer. Al looks up at her.

Karen: "There was nothing to tell."
Al: "You deliberately led me into a trap."
Karan: "Al, you're talking senselessly. What do you mean by that?"
Al: "You knew I was falling in love with you . . . and you said you loved me."

Karen: "I said I was fond of you. There's a difference between what I said and what you thought I said."
Al: "Don't holler at me. I'm not deaf."

There is a silence again.

Al: "I'm sorry, Karen. I just blew up. Let's forget about what happened tonight . . . alright?"
Karen: "I don't want to see you anymore, Al."
Al: "Don't say that, Karen. This is just a big mistake. I love you too much to lose you. If I had to go through life without you, I'd blow my brains out."
Karen: "It's over and finished."
Al: "Karen, let's talk this over. We can . . ."
Karen: "Get out and don't come back." She starts to walk toward the front door. Al grabs her by the throat in anger.
Al: "You can't throw me out like a piece of shit."

Karen is gasping for air.

Al: "You know who I am?"

Karen gasps for air. "I—can'-t—bre-athe!"
Al realizes what he's doing and withdraws the pressure on her throat and lets her go. Karen staggers to the couch with her hand on her throat, coughing.
Al has come to his senses and says, "I don't think you're really worth it," and leaves.
Karen is now feeling better.

The next morning Leach is having breakfast with Bell.

Leach: "I'm glad you took the day off, Bell. This means a lot to me."
Bell: "Well, you sounded very convincing on the phone this morning, Leach. Now what was so important?"
Waitress: "More coffee?"
Bell: "No, thank you."
Leach: "Well, what I had in mind was skipping all the formalities and getting right to the point." Then he just stares at Bell.
Bell: "Well . . . get to the point."
Leach: "Will you marry me . . . please?"

Bell: "Oh, Leach, you don't know how happy I am that you asked me that. Yes, I will marry you."

Leach: "You make me feel ten feet tall saying that, Bell." He looks at his watch. "It's after nine. The stores are open. Let's go get the rings."

Bell reaches for his hand and smiles. "O.K."
Leach and Bell enter the jewelry store. The jeweler approaches them.

Jeweler: "Good morning. Can I help you?" (to Leach)

Leach: "Yes, I want to buy my fiancee an engagement ring and a wedding band."

Jeweler: "What price range did you have in mind, sir?"

Leach: "Well, something not too cheap. About $40,000."

Bell looks at Leach in a very surprised way.

Jeweler: "Are you going to have this financed with a bank, sir?"

Leach: "No, it's going to be cash. I'll have the money for you at noon."

Jeweler: "Very good, sir." He goes to get a tray of diamonds.

Bell: "Leach, what are you talking about? $40,000! You don't make that much in two years."

Leach: "Please, Bell, let me handle this."

Belle puts her hands on her hips. "*Leach!*"

Jeweler: "Here you are, sir, a great selection."

Leach: "Oh, thank you. Which one do you like, Bell?"

Bell just rolls her eyes up in the air like it was a joke and looks at the tray of diamonds and picks out a pair. "These are nice."

Jeweler: "Those are $42,000."

Bell: "Oh no, we don't want those."

Leach: "Oh yes, we do. Measure her finger and get them ready and we'll pick them up at noon.

They exit the store.
They are walking down the sidewalk.

Bell: "Wait a minute, Leach. I love you and I want to marry you, but I think you've flipped out. How are you going to pay for those rings?"

Leach:	"Bell, I have a confession to make to you. But before I tell you . . . look, I love you very much and you do want to marry me, don't you?"
Bell:	"Yes, Leach, I do. I love you."
Leach:	"Well . . . I'm a millionaire."
Bell:	"Oh my God, you've really flipped out." She puts her hand to her forehead.
Leach:	"No Bell, it's true. So are Eddy and Al. We didn't want anyone to know."
Bell:	"Why?"
Leach:	"I wanted to meet a lady like you. I thought if you knew I was a millionaire, you'd marry me for my money."
Bell:	"You know better than that."
Leach:	"I do now. Guess what."
Bell:	"Tell me."
Leach:	"I have a big house in Malibu."
Bell:	"Oh, Leach, no more surprises for today. I've had enough excitement."
Leach:	"O.K. Let's go to the bank."

Bell rolls her eyes and puts her hand to her head, saying, "Oh boy."

Clara is walking to work. Eddy is already there, standing on the balcony of the hotel watching Clara go to work. They see each other during the day but do not speak to each other for some time. Eddy starts to drink heavily in his spare time, not eating proper meals and losing about 25 pounds. Then one night he goes to Clara's apartment. He knocks on her door. Clara answers the door.

Clara:	"What do you want?"
Eddy:	"I just wanted to say hello. Just wanted to see how you were doing."
Clara:	"You can't come in."
Eddy:	"I don't want to come in."

They just look at each other for a few seconds and Clara kind of turns her head away from him.

Eddy:	"I, ah . . . . was in the area. I thought I'd stop by and say hi."
Clara:	"You're repeating yourself."
Eddy:	"Uh, I'm a little mixed up . . . I still love you, Clara."
Clara:	"I don't want to hear it."
Eddy:	"I want you to hear it. After all, I'm in love with you."
Clara:	"I didn't tell you to fall in love with me."
Eddy:	"No. But you were aware of it. You should have said something . . . anything to discourage me. I feel hurt . . . and betrayed."

Clara:	"I don't care how you feel after you spyed on me."
Eddy:	"I didn't spy on you. You know what you are?"

Clara doesn't say anything, just looks at him.

Eddy:	"You know what you are?"
Clara:	"What am I?"
Eddy:	"You're a . . ." He stops talking and just looks at her, slowly looks away from her, then looks at her again. "I'm sorry . . . I'm sorry."
Clara:	"I've got to go." She slowly starts to close the door.
Eddy:	"Don't close the door on me, Clara."
Clara:	"I've got to go." She slowly closes the door on Eddy.

Eddy goes to his camper and goes to sleep. The next day which is his day off he gets up early and waits for Clara to go to work. He waits about half a block from her apartment. About twenty minutes later she leaves her apartment and walks toward him. When she reaches him Eddy says, "Good morning, Clara."

Clara doesn't say anything. Eddy starts to walk with her.

Eddy:	"Look, Clara, I know I've been acting like a fool and I had no right to act like that. Maybe we could be friends."

Clara looks at him as they are walking.

Eddy:	"I mean it—just friends. Look, from now on if I come over to your house and you have some guy there, just tell me and I'll leave, O.K.? I just want to be friends, O.K.? Will you stop a minute? Please."
Clara:	"I don't believe you."
Eddy:	"I have no reason to lie to you. If you don't want to be friends it's up to you. I'm hoping we could be."

Clara just looks at him.

Eddy:	"O.K . . . . O.K.?
Clara:	"Alright, alright. I have to get to work." She starts to walk away.
Eddy:	"You gonna be home tonight?"

Clara turns but keeps on walking.

Clara:	"No, I'm going somewhere."

Eddy: "That's all right. I'll see you some other time." And he looks at her as she walks to work. Then he starts to walk back to his truck and sees a beautiful lady riding a horse on the beach. She's wearing a bikini.

Al has quit his job and is not responding too well to other people. He drinks heavily and is really heartbroken. He goes to Avila to find Eddy. But Eddy is nowhere in sight. Then Al goes to Leach's house and Leach is out. He can't get ahold of Leach either.

Al just wanders from bar to bar. He calls Karen and the phone rings four times.

Karen: "Hello."

Al: "Hi, it's me. I was wondering if I could come over for a while."

Karen: "You have a lot of nerve calling here, Al. It's been three days and I still have bruises on my neck."

Al: "I'm sorry, Karen, I just went out of my mind."

Karen: "You're lucky I didn't call the cops, Al."

Al: "Look, Karen, I said I'm sorry. I have to talk to you. Could I come over?"

Karen: "No. I don't want you over here. I'm going out tonight."

Al: "With who?"

Karen: "It's none of your business who I go out with. Don't call here again." And she hangs up.

Al is even more broken up. now. At times his mind was thoughtless. He was very much in love with Karen. Karen was an angel that didn't care if Al exited or not. She had been seeing other men all the time. That night Al continues to drink into the early morning hours and finally passes out in his car.

The next day Leach and Bell are driving to Al's house.

Leach: "How do you like the rings, Bell?"

Bell: "I love them, Leach. I just adore them." She smiles.

Leach: "Well they didn't give me much for my old junk but that's all right. You like the car too, Bell?" It's a brand new Mercedes Benz.

Bell: "Yes, I like these two seaters. I wonder if Al will be home."

Leach: "I don't know. I've been trying to get ahold of Al and Leach for two days. Al doesn't answer his phone and Eddy hasn't checked with his answering service. Well, maybe they're just busy. But if we don't find them this morning they're going to miss a good wedding at noon. That's his apartment. I don't see his car."

Bell:	"Are you going to see if he's there?"
Leach:	"Yeah, we'll check it out."

They park the car and go to Al's apartment door and knock. There is no answer.

Bell:	"Where could he be at?"
Leach:	"I have no idea. Let's go."

On their way back to the car a lady and her little girl are about to enter an apartment three doors from Al's.

Leach:	"Excuse me, do you know Al who lives in number 1C? Have you seen him?"
Lady:	"Yes, I know him but he hasn't been home in four days.
Leach:	"Four days."
Lady:	"I'm sorry."
Leach:	"Thank you."

On their way back to the car Leach says, "He's probably in Avila with Eddy. We'll stop by and see if we can find them."

Leach and Bell are now going through the main street in Avila.

Leach:	"Well, this is the third time we came down this street and I don't see Al's car or Eddy's pickup."
Bell:	"What are we going to do?"
Leach:	"I'm sorry, Bell, but we can't wait any longer. It's 11:15."
Bell:	"I'm sorry, Leach. I know you wanted your friends to be there."
Leach:	"Well, we tried."

At the chapel there were only two witnesses, the preacher's wife and Bell's sister, of course.

Preacher:	"Do you, Bell Stockwell, take this man, Leach Morgan, as your lawful wedded husband?"
Bell:	"I do."
Preacher:	"Do you, Leach Morgan, take this woman, Bell Stockwell, as your lawful wedded wife?"
Leach:	"I do."
Preacher:	"I now pronounce you man and wife."

Leach and Bell look at each other and kiss.

Bell's sister, Sandy, says, "I'm so happy for you, Bell," and kisses her on the cheek. She looks at Leach and says, "Congratulations, Leach."

Leach: "Thank you, Sandy."
Preacher: "My blessings, my son."
Preacher's wife: "Contratulations, too, both of you. You make a wonderful couple."
Bell: "Thank you very much, Mrs. Prescott, thank you so much."

That night they have a party at the Hungry Tiger. Leach has rented the bottom lounge and dining area. They have champagne, lobster, prime rib, oysters—you name it, they have it. Everybody is dancing, laughing, eating, having a good time when one of the musicians says over the microphone, "Listen up, everybody, listen up. We have a request that we play a classic for the newlyweds. How about it, huh?"

Crowd: "Yuh *Yahhyay!*"
Leach: "I guess it's our dance, Bell."

Bell looks at him, smiles and says, "I guess it is."

They walk to the middle of the floor and a German waltz is played. They dance superbly, looking at each other straight in the eye all through the dance with a slight smile. Some of the crowd stares in sadness, others with a slight smile, and others with tears in their eyes. The song is over and the crowd cheers and cheers.

That night Eddy went to Avila, just being curious about Clara. It's 2 A.M. Eddy passes in front of her apartment but does not stop or toot the horn. The lights in her apartment are on. He parks his truck at the Bay Inn where he works. He looks down at Clara's apartment, wondering what her lights are doing on so late. He sits there and waits and waits. About an hour later he sees a guy come out of the apartment and leave in a small sports car. Ten minutes later a white Corvette comes down the street from her apartment. The guy leaves his car and walks to her place and knocks at her door. She answers the door immediately and he is in the apartment before you can say two shakes. Eddy cannot believe his eyes. He looks at his watch. It is 2:45 A.M. He waits and watches. When the guy leaves it is 3:30 A.M. Ten minutes later her lights go out. Eddy sits in his truck till dawn, then goes to another nearby town to get away from things.

Al is now on his way to Avila, unshaven, his hair uncombed and sipping whiskey from a pint bottle. Al and Eddy pass each other on Avila Road but have no idea that they did; because of their tragedies their minds are not fully aware of what they are doing.

Al is mumbling to himself. "Goddamn whore . . . bitch." He takes a sip of whiskey. Tears run down his face. "Sniff, sniff, Goddamn it, I love you Karen." He starts to cry.

Al starts to come into the town of Avila. He pulls into town and parks. He pulls himself together and looks around. The streets are empty. It's early in the morning and no one is up yet. It's six in the morning. He spots a phone across the street. He gets out of his car and goes to the phone to call Karen. He dials her number and the phone rings six times.

Al: "Come on, Karen, answer the phone."

It rings three more times and he hears her phone lifted off the receiver and a man's sleepy voice says, "Hello, hello. Who is this? Hello." And the man hangs up. Al does not say anything. He just stares down the street with tears coming out of his eyes. He hangs up the phone, crosses the street and walks along the beach.

Leach: "Good morning, Mrs. Morgan."
Bell: "Good morning, Mr. Morgan."

Leach kisses Bell and embraces her. Twenty minutes elapse.

Leach: "Come on, get up. I'm taking you to Los Angeles this afternoon. I'm going to show you your new home."
Bell: "Is it beautiful, Leach?"
Leach: "It's one of the best in Beverly Hills—swimming pool, tennis court, you name it, you got it."

They're now having breakfast in a restaurant in Morrow Bay.

Leach: "I have so many things to do when I get to L.A."
Bell: "Like what for instance, Leach?"
Leach: "Well, I know I have a couple of films I have to produce plus look over some contracts for a starter."
Bell: "Is there any way I can help?"

Leach: "Yes, there is, love. You'll be working with me constantly until you learn the ropes. Then you can help me with half the business. Just for a while I want you to know what's going on."

Bell: "Are we going straight to Los Angeles from here when we leave?"

Leach: "I thought we'd stop in Avila to check on Al and Eddy just to see if they're there. I want to let them know that we're going back."

Bell smiles. "That's fine with me."

Eddy had not been drinking much that morning. He's now in a bar called the King of Clubs, playing pool with a lady. The lady has just made the eight ball.

Eddy: "Well, I never lost four games in a row before."

Lady: "There's always a first time for everything, Mister."

Eddy: "You're telling me, baby." He rubs his forehead. "You want to have breakfast with me?"

Lady: "Sure . . . I'll have breakfast with you."

Al is now about a mile north of Avila, still walking on the beach approaching a pier. From time to time his lips tighten and his mouth curves down like he is going to cry. He climbs up on the main road to get to the pier. He isn't even responding to one or two cars that pass by. He is lost now without Karen. He comes upon the pier and walks a few feet toward the end of the pier. It is a few minutes past noon now. He stares at the skyline and the water line for a few seconds. Tears roll down his face. His lips tighten as if he's going to cry aloud but he holds it in. He walks a few more feet and finds some old chains that fishermen use to anchor their boats. He picks one up and climbs the bannister of the pier. Across the way is a small beach. About a quarter of a mile away a young man and a young lady are bathing in the sun by the shore, drinking beer.

Lady: "Look at that guy on the pier. What's he doing?"

Man: (not looking) "He's going to do some fishing. What else?" He kisses her on the shoulder and back.

Lady: "No, look. I'm serious."

Al has wrapped the chain around him securely. The pier is empty except for some people at the end of the pier. Al looks at the water below without any expression on his face and jumps.

Lady on beach: "*Yaah*! Oh my God!"

Man: "Goddamn! Let's get over there. Come on."

The lady and man start to run along the beach toward the pier, hollering at people in their campers and others just lounging in the sun in their chairs.

Man: "A guy just jumped off the pier! Come on, give me a hand! Somebody call an ambulance!"

Everybody starts to run toward the pier. They come to the spot where Al jumped off.

Man: "I'm diving in."
Lady: "Be careful."

The young man dives in, penetrating the water with force. Everyone is looking with wide eyes and commotion. The young man disappears for about thirty seconds, then surfaces.

Young man:"He's to heavy. I can't pull him up. He dives down again.

Forty-five minutes elapse. The ambulance is there and has broght Al up. Al is now in the ambulance, dead. The ambulance attendant is taking reports from different people.

Leach and Bell are now entering the town of Avila and driving along the waterfront street.

Leach: "There's Al's car." He parks across the street from Al's car. "Come on, Belle, I want you to meet my friend. He shouldn't be too far off."

They look in the restaurants and bars and on the beach but can't find Al.

Leach: "I wonder where he could be."

Bell just shakes her head in disappointment.

Leach: "Let's go back to his car and wait."

They hear some people telling their friends, "Did you hear about that guy that drowned at the last pier?"

Friend: "No, what happened?"
Other friend:"I'm not sure. This guy jumped off the pier and drowned."

Leach: "Excuse me, do you know the name of this guy?"
Man: "No sir, I don't. I just heard about it."
Leach: "Thank you." He says to Bell, "I think we'd better look into this just
           to be safe."

A sheriff's car passes by and Leach waves him down.

Leach: "Excuse me, officer, I heard there was an accident on the other end
           of town."
Officer: "Yes, there was. You think you know him?"
Leach: "I don't know. I'd like to know his name if possible."
Officer: "Sure, I don't see any harm in that." He reaches for his report. "Let me see
           now. His name is Al . . . Al . . . . Al Strosiky. He drowned about 12:30."

Leaches eyes widen with shock. "Drowned!"

Bell: "Oh my God!"
Leach: "What happened?"
Officer: "We took different reports from different people and one report kind
           of stood out. This guy that knew him said he'd been having trouble
           with his girl."
Leach: "Trouble? What kind of trouble?"
Officer: "Well . . . (tipping his hat to Belle) Excuse me, ma'am. This guy said
           this Al guy found out his girl was a whore."

Leach looks at Bell. Bell looks down.

Officer: "I guess it was too much for him to take . . . that wasn't the easy way
           out, you know . . ."
Leach: "Thank you, officer . . . thank you." He reaches for Bell's arm and
           walks back to the sidewalk. "Al's dead. How could this be possible?"
           He looks at Bell in disbelief.
Bell: "What can we do?"
Leach: "We can't do anything."

Eddy passes by in his truck and says, "Hey, Leach . . ."
Leach kind of yells, "Eddy, park your truck and come here."
Eddy parks his truck and makes his way back to Leach and Bell.

Eddy: "What's up, Leach? Good to see you."
Leach: "Al's dead."

Eddy: "Dead? What are you talking about?"
Leach: "He jumped off the pier about three hours ago and drowned."
Eddy: "You mean suicide?"

Leach nods his head yes.

Eddy: "Why would he do something stupid like that?"
Leach: "The sheriff's report said he found out his girl was a whore."

Eddy looks toward the ocean and says, "Poor devil . . . I know it's tough but he had no call to do that." His eyes turn red.

Leach: "Look, let's pull ourselves together. I'm sorry, Bell."
Bell: "That's alright, Leach."
Leach: "Eddy, this is my wife, Belle. Bell, this is my friend, Eddy."
Eddy: "I'm pleased to meet you, Bell."
Bell: "It's nice to meet you, Eddy."
Leach: "Where's your girl?

Eddy exhales and says, "I have no girl . . . . she turned out to be a whore, too."

Bell: "Oh Eddy, I'm so sorry." She reaches for his arm.
Eddy: "Thanks, Bell. I guess I haven't got the sense to do what Al did."
Leach: "Come on, let's cut that shit out. What happened, Eddy?"
Eddy: "She fooled me right down to the last card. Her smile was so innocent.
           She was going to church all the time. She played the part so well.
           Her eyes, they looked like they were from an angel . . ." Then Eddy
           looked at Leach and Bell. "An angel in disguise."

At that moment Tony, the chauffeur, comes around the corner in a Cadillac convertible with three beautiful girls.

Eddy: "Look who in the hell is coming up the street."
Leach: "Tony. What the hell is he doing here?"
Eddy: "I don't know." Eddy waves him down. "What the hell are you doing
           here, Tony?"
Tony: "The girls missed you and were worried about you and they wanted
           to see you, and you said to give them a ride to wherever they wanted
           to go, so here we are."
Eddy: "Well I'll be damned. How perfect can things be timed?"

Leach: "Eddy, Bell and I are going back to L.A. Need a ride?"
Eddy: "No thanks, Leach. Goodbye, Bell."
Bell: "Goodbye, Eddy."

Leach and Bell leave.

Eddy: "Well, you girls look more beautiful now than the last time I saw you."

The girls giggle. One of the girls says, "Eddy, you haven't changed at all."
Clara is in her apartment across the street and looks out the window and sees Eddy across the street. She goes out of the apartment and closes the door and stands there looking at Eddy."
Eddy; "Well, girls, I'm going to take you all to dinner." He spots Clara across the street. "Excuse me, girls, I'll be right back."
Eddy crosses the street to where Clara is standing.

Eddy: "I was hoping I'd see you before I left."
Clara: "Where are you going?"
Eddy: "Back to L.A. My business is finished here."
Clara: "Business?"
Eddy: "It's a long story, Clara. Maybe someday I'll see you again. Goodbye."
Clara: "Eddy, I know now that I love you."

Eddy looks at her with a very small smile and looks away from her, kind of looking at the ground. He takes two steps back, kind of turning around, then looks at her and says, "I still love you, Clara," and he goes to the car.
When he gets to the car one of the girls says, "Who was that?"
Eddy looks at Clara across the street then back to the girl and smiles.

Eddy: "Just an angel, my love, just another angel," and they all leave in the car.

Clara watches them disappear in the crowded street never to see Eddy again.

THE END